A DANGEROUS GAME

MALORIE BLACKMAN

Barrington Stoke

For Neil and Elizabeth, with love

First published in 2018 in Great Britain by
Barrington Stoke Ltd
18 Walker Street, Edinburgh, EH3 7LP

www.barringtonstoke.co.uk

This text was first published in a different form as
Forbidden Game (Puffin Books, 1994)

Text © 1994 Oneta Malorie Blackman
Illustration © 2018 Mike Lowery

The moral right of Oneta Malorie Blackman and Mike Lowery
to be identified as the author and illustrator of this work has
been asserted in accordance with the Copyright, Designs and
Patents Act, 1988

A CIP catalogue record for this book is available
from the British Library upon request

ISBN: 978-1-78112-823-7

Printed in China by Leo

CONTENTS

Chapter 1

I Told You

"*Come on, Sam*," said Billy. "Show them you can do it."

The cheers and jeers of the crowd around Sam were so loud that he could only just hear his best friend Billy. Sam tried to ignore the frantic beat of his heart slamming against his ribs. He tried to ignore the deafening noise all around him. Instead, he forced himself to focus on his arms. Big mistake! The muscles in Sam's upper arms felt like they'd locked solid and caught fire!

"*Come on, Sam!*" Billy's yells were even more urgent now.

"What a wimp!" said another voice. "Look at the sweat dropping off his forehead. He's only done four press-ups and he's ready to pass out."

Sam didn't need to look up to know who'd just spoken. Brandon.

I am not a wimp, Sam thought. *I'll show you, maggot-face! I can do this, I know I can. I just need to* push! Sam tried to relax his arm muscles a tiny bit – so that they'd unlock without the rest of his body crashing to the floor.

Push!

Sam gritted his teeth so hard they felt like they'd shatter at any second. He tried to force his arms to push the rest of his body upwards. At that moment, Sam felt as if he had an adult elephant sitting on his back. His mum was always nagging him about how skinny he was and how he needed to put on more weight to become stronger. But Sam didn't feel the least bit strong right then!

"Almost, Sam. Almost," screamed Billy. He sounded like he was about to burst a blood vessel. But Sam had never been so grateful for the sound of Billy's voice.

He could do it ... *He could do it ...*

He couldn't!

Sam collapsed in a heap on the gravel below him. A sharp piece of stone dug into his chin, but Sam didn't even wince. No matter how much his chin might hurt, it couldn't compare to how awful he felt inside. He'd failed.

"Oh!" The crowd around him gave a disappointed sigh – as if Sam had let them all down as well. He turned his head. Some of them were drifting away already. Others were looking at him and shaking their heads.

"I told you he wouldn't be able to do five press-ups," Brandon sneered. "I'm surprised he could manage four."

"Shut up, Brandon," snapped Billy. "Sam did his best."

"His best isn't up to much," Brandon replied. "His best is less than my worst!"

"Leave him alone," said Billy. "He's only just got over being ill ..."

"When is he going to stop using that as an excuse for being so useless?" Brandon said, unimpressed.

Sam wished his friend would shut up. He knew that Billy was only standing up for him, but it wasn't making him feel any better. In fact, it was just the opposite – Billy was making him feel worse. Sam had his breath back now and scrambled to his feet. Brandon and his friends stood in a line, looking at Sam like he was something disgusting they'd just stepped in. He knew what they were thinking: he was a weed, a weakling, a waste of space. And in that moment, Sam felt that they were right.

"Are you boys planning to sleep here tonight?" the caretaker called from the school entrance. "Or will you be going home some time before I retire?"

Brandon and his friends left without looking back. And just like that, Sam was dismissed. Sam brushed the gravel off his hands, wishing they were the only part of his body that hurt.

"Never mind them," Billy said with a smile. "You did great."

"No, I didn't." Sam shook his head. "I couldn't even do five press-ups. Five rotten press-ups. My mum could do more than that!"

"It doesn't matter," Billy told Sam. "It's not important—"

"It is to me," Sam interrupted.

"You're making mountains out of molehills. It was just a silly game—"

"A silly game that I couldn't even finish," sighed Sam. "You know what? I don't blame Brandon for not liking me much. The only game I'm good for is tiddlywinks – that's what everyone thinks. I can't do anything. I don't go anywhere – I'm not even going on the school trip to Loch Lomond."

"So you didn't get your mum and dad to change their minds?" Billy asked.

"I didn't even try. What's the point?" Sam sighed. "I know what they will say."

"They might surprise you," said Billy.

"Yeah, and we might get blue snow tomorrow," Sam sniffed. And he knew which one was more likely. When they'd first been told about the school trip, Sam's mum and dad had both left a loud "*No*" ringing in his ears. Sam pursed his lips. He was fed up of spending his life watching others enjoy themselves while he sat on the sidelines. He wasn't going to do it any more. He *wasn't*.

"I'm going to ask Mum and Dad again tonight," Sam told Billy. "And this time I'm not going to take no for an answer."

"Good luck!" said Billy, his tone dry.

"Thanks," Sam replied. "I'm going to need it."

*

"You never let me do anything," Sam said to his parents that evening. "You won't let me try out for my school's athletics team. You won't let me play football or go swimming. I wouldn't even know how to swim if Uncle John hadn't taught me. And now you won't let me go on the school trip."

Dad lowered his newspaper, and Sam saw the wrinkles on his dad's forehead deepen into a frown. "Sam, don't talk to us like that. We're doing it for your own good."

"Don't you understand?" Sam pleaded. He could feel this argument was about to end the same way they always did. "You and Mum wrap me up in so much cotton wool, I'm suffocating."

"That's not true ..." Mum protested.

"Yes, it is," said Sam. He was almost shouting now. "I might as well stay in bed all day, every day and not do anything – ever again. What's the point of me even going to school if you're just going to treat me like a baby all the time? Why don't you just keep me chained and locked up in the attic? That way you'd know where I was and what I was doing every second of your lives."

"That's enough," Dad said. His newspaper lay forgotten on his lap.

"Sam, you're not being fair," Mum sighed. "We're only thinking of you and your health. We're not doing it on purpose, just to spoil your fun."

Sam didn't answer. What was he meant to say to that?

You might not be doing it on purpose, Mum, but you are ruining my life ...

"It's just that we have to do all we can to keep you well and out of hospital," Mum continued. "You don't want to go in again, do you? That's why we don't think the school trip to Scotland is a good idea. What if you ended up in hospital so far away from us?"

"I won't go into hospital, Mum. I promise," Sam pleaded. He didn't dare blink. His mum's face was now all blurred and swimming as unwanted tears filled his eyes. But there was no point crying – it wouldn't get him anywhere. Sam could just hear his mum now.

"*Don't run, Sam, you'll end up in hospital … Don't swim, Sam, you'll end up in hospital … Don't sulk, Sam, you'll end up in hospital … Don't cry, Sam, you'll end up in hospital …*"

"I never get to do anything," Sam sniffed as he turned around to leave the sitting room. "I might as well be dead."

Sam heard his mum gasp behind him, but he kept walking. He could have turned back and said he didn't mean it, but he would be lying.

Chapter 2

A Blue Tartan Sky!

Sam lay in bed that night, staring up at the ceiling and wishing that his parents would change their minds. All he could think about was the trip to Loch Lomond. He'd never been to Scotland before. He'd hardly been anywhere – not outside England, just a few times outside London, and never abroad.

A few years ago, Sam had asked his mum why they never went abroad for their holidays.

"What would happen if you got sick?" Mum replied.

That was her answer for everything. Anyone would think he was ill every minute of every day. OK, so he had to go into hospital sometimes. He couldn't help that. But when he wasn't in hospital, why couldn't he do all the things his classmates did?

Sam knew that when he wasn't in hospital, his mum thought it was only a matter of days (or maybe even hours) before he went in. That was all he was to his mum and dad – a boy who was ill in hospital or on his way to getting ill and would end up there.

"It's not fair," Sam mumbled as he stared at the ceiling.

Every break time, Sam did all the things his classmates did. He ran and played football just like them. Well, that wasn't strictly true. Sam was always the goalie – but he was good at it! Not that he'd ever tell his mum that – if he did, she'd be up at the school to complain.

"It's not fair," Sam whispered again.

And he fell asleep.

His dreams were full of the school trip to Loch Lomond. In his dreams he roller-bladed and abseiled and swam. He did all the things he'd always wanted to do, with no trouble at all. He dreamed of the hotel room he'd stay in for the five-night trip. It was a beautiful room with a grey tartan carpet and a yellow tartan duvet. When he'd looked out of the windows, the sky was blue tartan and the trees were green tartan. It was a wonderful dream!

But that was all it was – a dream.

Sam still had Scotland on his mind when he woke up the next morning. He wanted to stop thinking about it. Thinking about it just made him feel worse. He wasn't going to Scotland. He wasn't going anywhere. Today was the last day the money for the trip could be handed in.

Sam had his shower, then got dressed for school. He glanced in the mirror as he tucked his shirt into his trousers. In the mirror, he looked so normal.

"I am normal," Sam said as he frowned at his reflection.

His short hair was cut into a pattern at the sides and back of his head. He had dark-brown eyes, as dark as his skin. An average, normal boy. So why couldn't his parents treat him like that? When they looked at him, it was like all they could see was his illness. Sam walked slowly downstairs.

"Morning, Sam," Dad said with a smile.

"Hi, Dad," Sam said, and sat down to eat his breakfast.

It was cornflakes with hot milk, plus toast with thick orange marmalade, but Sam wasn't hungry. Dad got up to pour himself another black coffee. Sam looked down at his bowl of cornflakes. There had to be a way of going on the school trip – there just had to be. But even if Sam had the money to pay for the school trip himself – which he hadn't – Mum and Dad still had to sign the permission slip. How could he get round that? And even if he did manage it, there was no way he could be away for five days without Mum and Dad knowing.

"Sam, about this trip to Scotland …" Mum began.

Sam didn't bother to look up. "I know what you're going to say," Sam said. "You're sorry, but I can't go. There's no need to repeat yourself."

"That's where you're wrong," Mum said.

Sam looked up. He stared at his mum and dad. They were smiling at him. Sam hardly dared to breathe. Had he misheard? He must have done.

"Your dad and I have been talking it over ..." Mum continued.

"I can go?" Sam could only just get the words out.

Mum nodded and said, "You can go."

"You mean it? I can go?" Sam asked again. He sprang out of his chair and knocked it over.

Mum and Dad looked at each other and grinned.

"Yes, you can go," Dad said. "But only if you're really careful and you—"

"I'll be the most careful I've ever been in my life!" Sam told them as he beamed. "Yes! I can go. *I can go!*"

Sam gobbled down his breakfast and pretty much ran all the way to school. He burst into his classroom and saw his teacher Mrs Jenkins talking to another pupil. Sam hovered by her table, wanting to tell her his good news.

"The toilets are at the end of the corridor, Sam," Mrs Jenkins said, and raised her eyebrows at him.

"Huh?" Sam said.

"Isn't that why you're hopping from foot to foot?" Mrs Jenkins said.

Sam grinned at her. "No, miss," he said. "It's about the trip to Scotland. My mum and dad gave me the money, and they've signed the form and everything. I can go!"

Chapter 3

Sam's Such a Wimp!

After assembly, the only thing anyone could talk about was the school trip. Today was Monday. So in just four more days, they'd be off! The coach was going to leave just after Friday's assembly and would arrive in Loch Lomond on Friday night. Just in time for a late dinner. They would be returning home on Wednesday morning, which meant they'd have the whole of Saturday, Sunday, Monday and Tuesday in Scotland. Five whole wonderful, glorious, marvellous, fantastic, brilliant days away from home!

"Can I have some quiet, please?" Mrs Jenkins shouted from the front of the classroom. "I can't hear myself think."

The noise in the class died to a low rumble. Mrs Jenkins took off her glasses and polished them on the front of her blouse.

"Right, then," Mrs Jenkins said. "I've got the groups for Saturday's trek in Queen Elizabeth Forest. And before anyone asks – no, you cannot change your groups. Molly, Charlotte, Nevin, Fadia – you're in the Red group."

Billy elbowed Sam in the ribs.

"I hope we're in the same group," Billy whispered.

"So do I," Sam replied, and crossed his fingers.

"Joe, David, Mahendra, Scott – you're in the Blue group," Mrs Jenkins continued. "Brandon, Tayo, Jack, Sam, you're in Green—"

"Oh, miss, do we have to have Sam?" said Brandon.

"Yeah, Mrs Jenkins!" Jack added. "We don't want him."

The whole class went as silent as a graveyard. Sam's face began to burn. Everyone was watching him now – he could feel their eyes jabbing and stabbing into him.

"I already said you cannot change your groups," Mrs Jenkins snapped.

"But, miss, Sam's such a wimp ..." Brandon protested.

"And he's always ill ..." said Tayo.

"I don't want to hear another word out of any of you," Mrs Jenkins said. "Sam is in your group and that's final."

"But, miss …"

Mrs Jenkins raised her hand and added, "One more word and Sam will be the only person from the Green group going on this trip. Do I make myself clear? It'll be three fewer people for me to worry about."

Sam looked down – if he could have slunk under his desk without his teacher seeing, he would have done it. He looked up and regretted it. Tayo and Brandon were glaring at him.

It's not my fault, Sam thought. *I didn't ask to be in their group.* Sam tried to stare back at them, but it was like trying to outstare two hungry lions.

"Mrs Jenkins, can Sam be in my group?" Billy called out.

"No, he cannot," Mrs Jenkins said. "He's in the Green group, and that's the end of it." Mrs Jenkins' eyes blazed as she looked around the class. She continued reading out the groups.

"Thanks for trying," Sam said to Billy.

"Don't worry about Brandon and all that lot," Billy told Sam. "They're not worth it. Bunch of bullies. They think they're so tough."

"That's cos they are," Sam sighed to himself.

Not for the first time, Sam wished he didn't have sickle-cell. He wished he didn't get tired and out of breath so easily, and have the agony that came whenever he had a sickle-cell crisis.

"Right, everyone, get into your groups," Mrs Jenkins ordered.

Chair legs scraped across the wooden classroom floor with excited laughter and chatter.

"*With less noise, please!*" Mrs Jenkins yelled. "Sam, shift! Or are you waiting for me to carry you? Your group is over by the window."

Reluctantly, Sam went over to them. Brandon and Tayo were still glaring at him. Jack was looking anywhere but at him. Jack was all right by himself, but with the other two he was just as bad as they were.

"Don't worry," Sam hissed. "I don't want to be in this rotten group any more than you want me in it."

"Would you please all shush?" Mrs Jenkins shouted again over the noise swamping her. "I want you all to listen very carefully to these instructions. They're very important."

The noise died down.

"Thank you all so much," Mrs Jenkins said with sarcasm. "Now then, on Saturday afternoon we'll all be trekking through Queen

Elizabeth Forest. Every group will be with one adult. Each group will start from a different point in the forest, and you'll have to make your way to the central meeting place. You will be given maps and compasses to use. You won't be allowed to take phones – not even the adults – so don't think you'll be able to use GPS. Your route will be the path marked up on your map. None of you are to leave your group's path, whatever happens. Is that clear?"

"Yes, Mrs Jenkins," a few pupils muttered.

Sam glared at Tayo, thinking, *If you don't stop staring at me, I'm going to … to poke you in the eye!*

"Sam Norris, are you listening to me?" Mrs Jenkins asked.

"Yes, miss," Sam replied.

"Hmm!" Mrs Jenkins said. She walked up to Sam's group first.

"OK, Green group," Mrs Jenkins said. "There's your map and a compass. Your route is marked in green pen. You'll start three miles south of the meeting place, so all you have to do is follow the path northwards. The path twists and turns a bit, but as long as you follow it, you'll be fine. The compass needle always points north, so you can use that to guide you too. Even you lot couldn't get lost."

Mrs Jenkins moved on to the next group.

Sam bent his head to look at the green path. His group's starting point was almost directly south of the meeting place, and their route was a clear S-shape.

"Let's try to be the first ones back at the meeting place," Tayo said.

"Even if we have to run all the way to do it," Jack added.

Brandon turned to Sam and told him, "I'm going to look after the map and the compass, so you'd better keep up with us or you'll get lost."

Were they really going to run all the way? Sam shook his head. No. No way. Besides, the adult they'd have with them wouldn't allow it, would they?

"Don't worry. I'll keep up," Sam said. He felt confident that they'd been winding him up.

"You! Don't make me laugh," Tayo jeered. "We're going to be travelling so fast you won't see us for dust. You'll be all alone in the forest with the wolves and lynxes and the hungry wildcats ..."

"If you lot are trying to scare me," said Sam, "I'll tell you now, you're wasting your time."

Brandon and Tayo swapped a look that sent a chill snaking down Sam's spine. They were

up to something, planning something already –
Sam could tell.

"I'm not scared of you lot," Sam told them.
"Or your stupid made-up animals." He tried to
make his voice sound as cool as he could, but it
just came out all gruff, like he had a head cold.

"We'll see," Brandon replied. "We'll see."

Chapter 4

Loch Lomond

"Isn't this great?" Billy said as he climbed up the ladder to the top bunk.

"Hey!" Sam said. "I thought we agreed to toss a coin for the top bunk?"

"Worth a try," Billy said with a grin, and climbed down again.

Sam dug a ten pence coin from his pocket. "Heads or tails?" he asked.

"Er ... tails," said Billy.

Sam flicked the coin. He and Billy watched as it spun in the air.

"Heads," Sam said as he caught it. He thrust the coin towards Billy's nose. "I get the top bunk. Step aside!"

"Huh! Best of three?" Billy suggested.

"You must be nuts!" Sam climbed up the ladder.

Sam had never slept in a bunk bed before. He flopped down on the bed and let his feet dangle over the side. Brilliant! Sam looked across the room. The carpet was grey like rain clouds, and the duvet cover was plain blue. He thought back to his dream. No tartan in sight! But it didn't matter.

Sam couldn't stop grinning. He couldn't believe it. He was here, at last. It was all so fantastic. Even the long journey in the coach had been a laugh. They'd played games and sung songs and stopped five times – once to eat their packed lunches, the other times to go to the loo. He and Billy had sat next to each other and played hangman and battleships on their phones. Sam's first school trip – his first time away from home. Bliss! It was all so new and so different. He wished he could stay for longer than five days …

The bedroom door was flung open. Brandon, Tayo and Jack stood in the doorway.

"So this is where you are," Brandon said.

Sam's smile faded.

Tayo grinned and said, "We just wanted to remind you – the trek in Queen Elizabeth Forest is tomorrow."

"We don't need you to remind us," Billy said.

"Who's talking to you?" Brandon snapped. "We're talking to Sam. You'd better get a good night's sleep, wimp. You're going to need it."

And with that, Brandon and the others left the room, leaving the door wide open. Billy stomped over to it and slammed the door shut.

"What was that all about?" Billy asked Sam.

Sam shrugged and said, "I don't know. They're up to something, but I don't know what."

"Maybe you should tell Mrs Jenkins or one of the other teachers," Billy suggested.

"Tell them what?" asked Sam. "Brandon and the others haven't done anything … yet."

"You should talk to Mrs Jenkins anyway," Billy said.

"You must be joking!" Sam said. "I can't do that."

"Then what *are* you going to do?" Billy asked.

"I'll work that out when I know what they're up to," Sam told him. "Don't worry, I'm prepared – just in case they run off and leave me. Besides, the adult won't run off."

"Be careful," Billy said with a frown.

"Don't worry. I will be," Sam replied. "Besides, what can they do?"

Chapter 5

We're On Our Own

Saturday morning was wet and windy, but Sam didn't care. He was dressed in a shirt, two jumpers, blue anorak, jeans, two pairs of socks and his trainers, so he was as warm as toast and twice as happy!

The class spent the morning walking around Balloch Castle Country Park. Mrs Jenkins had given out a sheet of questions about the castle and its grounds that they all had to answer, but Sam didn't even mind that.

"Why did she give us so many questions to answer?" Billy grumbled next to Sam. "This is a Saturday, not a school day."

By lunch time it had stopped raining, but the sky was still dark grey. Mrs Jenkins looked up at the clouds.

"I hope it doesn't start to rain again or it'll ruin our day," Mrs Jenkins said to Mr Ford.

The class ate lunch in the grounds of the castle. The sun even popped out from behind a cloud, but not for very long.

"Has everyone got their maps and compasses?" Mrs Jenkins called out. "And your whistles to attract attention if something should happen?"

"Yes, miss ..." everyone replied.

Mrs Jenkins took another look up at the sky and said, "Right then. Before we all hop on the coach to Queen Elizabeth Forest, I want to remind you of a few things. *Stick to the paths.* If you leave your group's path, you'll get lost for sure. I shall go with the Lilac team to make sure you lot stay out of trouble. Mr Ford will walk with the Blue team and Mrs Isaac will be with the Purple team. You other teams already have your allocated adult. Mrs Tritton, could you take the Green team? And I'm warning all of you – I don't want any messing about. This is your chance to show whether or not you can be trusted."

Sam looked at Mrs Tritton. She was his classmate Fadia's mum, and she'd volunteered to come on the trip to help out.

She must be nuts! Sam decided.

He looked across to where the rest of his team were sitting. They were all grinning at him. Sam looked away fast. They didn't scare him. He dug his hand deeper into his anorak pocket to find the compass he'd bought with some of his savings. Holding it in his hand made him feel a lot better. Let them run off with the map if they wanted to. With his compass, he'd still find his way to the meeting place.

Everyone got on the coach, and they set off.

Ten minutes later, the coach stopped. Sam looked around. There was nothing but trees. It was as if the whole world had been swallowed up by trees. And they stood as tall and as frozen as statues.

"Blue team, you get off here," Mrs Jenkins said.

Mr Ford and his Blue group left the coach.

The giggles and whispers of excitement in the coach were getting louder and louder. As they set off again, Sam felt like he had a cricket ball sitting in his stomach. He'd never done anything like this before. He couldn't wait to get off the coach. He was looking forward to it, but at the same time he'd never been so nervous.

"OK, Green group," Mrs Jenkins said. "Off you get."

Sam stood up. He went to step out into the aisle of the coach but was pushed aside by the rest of his team.

"Watch it, you lot," Sam frowned at them.

"Watch it yourself," Brandon called back.

Sam looked down at Billy.

"Good luck, mate," Billy said with a smile. "See you later."

Sam nodded and moved down the aisle to the door.

"Remember, Green group – stick to the path," Mrs Jenkins reminded them.

"Miss, we're going to be the first ones at the meeting place," said Tayo. "You see if we're not."

Mrs Tritton got off the coach last. Seconds later, the coach vanished into a clump of trees.

"We're on our own now, miss," Brandon said to Mrs Tritton. "Isn't that great?!"

Sam didn't like the way Brandon was grinning at Mrs Tritton. Brandon was up to something. Sam knew it'd be something he wouldn't like. Something he wouldn't like at all.

Chapter 6

That's Not Right!

Sam zipped his anorak all the way up to his neck. The wind was cold in the forest, despite the sun doing its best to shine in a cloudy sky. Mrs Tritton asked them all their names, then she said, "OK, then, who's got the map?"

"I have, miss," Brandon replied.

Sam didn't like the way Brandon and Tayo grinned at each other. Mrs Tritton held one corner of the map, and Brandon held the other.

"That's our route, miss," said Tayo. He ran his finger along the route on the map marked out by the green pen.

Sam moved closer to get a better look. Something was wrong.

"That's not—" Sam began.

"That's not what?" Brandon said. His eyes blazed as he glared at Sam.

Sam looked at the map again. When Mrs Jenkins had given out the maps five days ago, his group's route had been S-shaped. Now it was a straight line from their starting spot to the meeting point at the centre of the forest. Sam looked at the other boys.

They'd changed the route. They must have bought a new map and drawn in a new green line.

"What were you going to say, Sam?" asked Mrs Tritton.

The others were scowling at him, daring him to tell Mrs Tritton. Sam dug his hand into his pockets to clasp his compass. The cold metal was oddly calming.

They had to be crazy to change the route like that. Mrs Jenkins had said they had to stick to their group's path.

What am I going to do? Sam thought.

He looked at Mrs Tritton, then at the rest of his group. They were staring at him now with cold, daring, angry eyes.

"I ... er ... nothing," Sam replied to Mrs Tritton at last.

Sam guessed changing the route had been Brandon's idea. As always, Brandon thought he knew best, and the rest followed like sheep.

"Come on, miss," said Brandon as he pushed the hair off his face. "We want to be the first ones back."

It was beginning to rain. It patted on the ground and splatted on the leaves of the trees around them. Apart from that, no other sound could be heard. Sam looked around. It was *so* quiet. Behind the rain, there was no sound at all.

Tayo took the group compass out of his pocket and said, "That's north, miss." He pointed.

Mrs Tritton folded up the map so that their route was showing on the outside and dropped it into a clear plastic bag to keep it dry. Then she peered down at the compass.

"OK, then," she said, and smiled at them all. "Let's get going."

They all started walking. Sam chewed on his bottom lip. What should he do? If he told Mrs Tritton what the others had done, then he knew they'd get in trouble – and they'd take it out on him. But if he said nothing, they might *all* get into trouble. Sam opened his mouth to speak, then snapped it shut again. He gripped the compass in his pocket tighter.

"Miss, can I see the map?" Sam asked.

Mrs Tritton handed it over. Sam took a good look at it. It didn't seem too bad. And anyway, how wrong could they go if they did leave the path? If they used the compass to go directly north, then they would meet up with the path in two places – once in the middle and again at the meeting place. And if they did leave the path, then they would be the first ones back. Sam looked up from the map and saw Jack was watching him. For a split second, Sam could have sworn that Jack wanted him to say something. But that was silly. Sam handed the map back to Mrs Tritton.

"All right, Sam?" Mrs Tritton asked.

"Fine, miss," Sam replied. "Just fine."

Mrs Tritton started chatting about when her family had gone for a trek in Breckon Woods.

"We all wanted to be adventurous and wade across the stream," Mrs Tritton said with a chuckle. "But I slipped and ended up taking a freezing cold bath in the water. Then I felt something icky and cold squirming around on my back. Let me tell you, I screamed like nothing you've ever heard. I pulled off my anorak and my jumper, and my husband had to put his hand down my back to get it out."

"And what was it?" Jack asked.

"A cold slippery fish," Mrs Tritton said. "I've never been able to eat or even look at any kind of fish again." She shivered at the thought.

Sam smiled up at her. Mrs Tritton was all right – for an adult. Fifteen minutes went by and then Brandon stopped walking and looked at the map.

"Mrs Tritton, the path runs to the east now," Brandon said. "We have to leave the path here and cut across through the trees."

"We do?" Mrs Tritton said. "Mrs Jenkins said we shouldn't leave the path."

"I guess we can, miss," Tayo said, "because our route's so easy."

Brandon smiled and added, "I think Mrs Jenkins meant that we're not to leave the path she drew on our maps."

"I'm not sure …" Mrs Tritton began. "I really don't think—"

"Have a look at the map, Mrs Tritton," Brandon interrupted, and he handed the map to her. "See!"

Mrs Tritton frowned down at the map, then looked at the compass, then went back to the map again.

She shrugged and said, "Well, that *is* the route Mrs Jenkins drew for us. So we'd better get going."

Sam looked at Brandon and Tayo, who were grinning at each other. He looked across at Jack. Jack looked how Sam felt – worried.

Chapter 7

Gunge and Mud

As they left the path, Sam looked back at it. He didn't want to take his eyes off it. But in less than a minute the path faded from a thin line to nothing at all. The rain falling off the leaves made plink-plink sounds on Sam's anorak hood. The noise sounded ten times louder in Sam's ears than he knew it really was.

And the rain wasn't stopping – it was growing heavier. Now that they'd left the proper path, the ground under their feet was getting slippery. To Sam, it felt like trying to walk through snow that had turned into a thick sludge. He had to make an effort to drag his feet out of the squelchy mud as he walked.

Tayo was holding the group compass now. Sam looked behind him. The forest looked the same no matter which way you turned. Trees and more trees. The path they'd been on had vanished.

"I'm not sure about this ..." Mrs Tritton said slowly. "Maybe we should turn back to try to find the path ..."

"We can't do that, Mrs Tritton," Brandon protested. "We'll never be the first ones at the meeting place if we turn back now."

"Well, Tayo, are you sure we're heading the right way?" Mrs Tritton asked.

"Yes, miss ..." Tayo said, but he didn't sound too sure.

Sam fell back behind everyone else and took out his own compass. Raindrops splashed on the glass front. Sam tilted the compass close to his face so that the rain ran off the glass. He gave a sigh of relief – they were still heading the right way.

They carried on walking. The trees seemed to be getting closer and closer together, and they were now climbing uphill. Sam felt horrible. Hot and sticky and damp. After twenty-five minutes, they were heading downhill. Sam took his compass out again.

"Are we still OK?" Jack asked, making Sam jump. He had appeared out of nowhere.

"I think so. So far ..." Sam replied.

So Jack was talking to him now!

"Shouldn't we have met up with the path by now?" Jack whispered.

Sam shrugged and said, "I don't have the map."

But Mrs Tritton must have thought the same as Jack. She stopped them all and asked to see the map again.

"According to this, we should hit the path at any moment now," Mrs Tritton said with a bright smile. A little too bright.

On they all went. Sam dreamed of taking off his wet clothes and having a long hot bath.

I wish it wasn't so muddy, he thought. *And I wish it'd stop raining – even for just a minute.*

No one was saying anything much now. Even Brandon and Tayo had shut up. Ten minutes later, they reached the path.

"Hooray!" Mrs Tritton shouted. "We're on the home stretch now. We'll soon be there."

Sam gave a great sigh of relief, and Jack too. The path was far easier to walk on. It was more solid, firmer, with less gunge and mud. Sam looked around. The path ran from south-east to north-west now.

"If we leave the path to go north now, the next time we get to the path we'll be at the meeting place," Tayo said.

Sam looked at Mrs Tritton, feeling horrified. Now that they'd reached the path, he didn't want them to leave it again. It might be slower, but it was safer and easier.

"Right then. Let's get going," Mrs Tritton said, and smiled. She looked at the map and checked the group compass, then pointed into the trees again. "That way."

Sam's heart sank into his toes. They'd got away with it the first time. Would they get away with leaving the path again?

Chapter 8

We're Lost!

Fifteen minutes after they'd left the path, they started travelling down a hill. The ground grew worse and worse. For the next twenty minutes, all they did was slip and slide and fall. The mud now seemed more like slippery ice. The wind began to howl around them like a screaming ghost, and the rain kept getting into everyone's eyes and blinding them.

Sam took out his compass, but huge droplets of rain covered the face. As soon as he had wiped them off, new ones would fall on the glass to take their place. Sam looked around.

He couldn't see much beyond the relentless grey curtain of rain. But he could see that they were halfway down the hill. Sam licked the rain off his lips and swallowed nervously. They'd come some way down. The trees weren't so packed together here. But the rain was still pouring down.

"As if we weren't wet enough," Sam muttered.

At least when they'd been further up, the trees had given them some shelter from the rain. Sam looked down the hill. The trees were closer together towards the bottom.

"Typical!" Jack said from next to him. "There's shelter everywhere apart from where we are!"

Sam smiled. Jack smiled back.

"Stop a minute, everyone," Mrs Tritton shouted over the roar of the wind. "I want to look at the map again."

They all stood in silence as Mrs Tritton studied it. She shook her head.

"We should have met up with the path again by now," Mrs Tritton said at last.

Brandon and Tayo swapped a look.

Yeah! You don't look so smart now, Sam thought with disgust.

Sam and the other boys watched each other, all of them waiting for someone else to speak.

"We're lost, miss, aren't we?" Jack shouted.

"According to the contour lines on this map, we should be heading uphill towards the path by now, not downhill," said Mrs Tritton.

"So we *are* lost," Sam said.

Mrs Tritton's lips thinned. "There's no need to panic," she said. "We'll be all right. I think we should retrace our steps back to the path and carry on from there."

"All the way back up that hill?" Tayo asked.

"Let's use our whistles. Maybe we're near another group," Mrs Tritton shouted, but she didn't sound like she believed it.

They all took out their whistles and blew as hard as they could. The sound was swallowed up by the wind and faded to nothing.

"If there is another team around here," Tayo said, "they'd have to be almost sitting on us to hear that." It was what they were all thinking.

Mrs Tritton drew herself up to her full height.

"Come on," she said. "Standing here isn't going to get us anywhere. Let's retrace our steps."

Sam looked up the hill. It hadn't seemed this steep when they'd been clambering down it.

"Now then, all link arms so that no one slips too far," Mrs Tritton suggested. "I'll go first."

Mrs Tritton held on to Brandon's arm, who in turn linked arms with Tayo. Then Tayo linked with Sam, who linked with Jack. Mrs Tritton started up the hill. For every step any of them took, they all slid back at least three steps.

After five minutes, Tayo straightened up. The wind lashed at them, and the rain hit them like slaps across the face.

"This isn't working," Tayo shouted. "We're wasting our time trying to get back up there. It's too slippery. There's nothing to hold on to."

Sam looked up at the dark grey sky. He'd never seen rain as bad as this. It was like each drop was at least a bucket's worth. Would it never ever stop?

"OK, then," Mrs Tritton shouted out. "Tayo, you keep blowing on that whistle. Blow every ten seconds or so. Understand? I'll keep the map. Jack, you look after the compass. I think that somehow we've gone too far north-east of the path and the meeting place."

Sam took out his own compass for another speedy look.

"We'll turn back down the hill," Mrs Tritton continued. "And then try to work our way to the west and south by going around it. Jack, you make sure that we keep travelling the same way until we get to the bottom of this hill.

Everyone keep your arms linked. Brandon, you lead the way and then Tayo. I'll go next and, Sam, you follow behind me. Jack, you can bring up the rear."

They set off, slipping down the hill. Sam could hardly hear Tayo's whistle over the wind and the rain, and he was not far behind him.

"Miss, I'll blow my whistle too," Sam said. "We'll have more chance of being heard that way."

"Good idea," said Mrs Tritton. "Go ahead."

Sam blew his whistle with Tayo. That was better! Much louder.

"Cheer up, everyone," Mrs Tritton shouted out. "We're going to be just fine. We're not going to be first, but we'll be fine. You'll see."

They carried on down the hill.

Then Sam heard a strange sound. A distant rumbling, rushing, roaring noise. It could be heard behind the howling wind and driving rain, but you had to listen carefully to separate the two similar sounds. Sam looked down the hill and could see nothing past the mass of tree trunks and leaves.

But something was definitely there. Something alarming. Something dangerous.

Chapter 9

Help Me!

"Mrs Tritton ..." Sam said, tapping her on the arm. "Mrs Tritton, there's something down there."

"Down where?" Mrs Tritton asked with a frown. She wiped rainwater off her soaking face.

Sam pointed. Tayo blew his whistle again.

"What's down there?" Jack shouted from behind Sam. "I can't hear anything."

The hill was getting steeper. They were all sliding rather than walking now.

"Miss! Miss! I think I see something," Brandon called out from the front.

"So do I!" Jack cried.

Brandon and Tayo stopped linking arms and pushed themselves forward to slide down the hill.

"There's something down there," Brandon shouted. Sam could only just hear him.

"Boys! *Stop!*" Mrs Tritton yelled.

"Miss ..." Jack said, and moved forward to follow the others.

Sam grabbed his arm. "No, don't," he said.

Mrs Tritton looked at Sam, her face grey with worry.

"We'd better get after them," Mrs Tritton said. "Link arms and don't let go, no matter what. *Brandon ... Tayo ...*"

Mrs Tritton, Sam and Jack struggled forward. The wind was behind them and pushed them on. They had to dig their heels into the mud and lean back to avoid sliding down too quickly.

Sam began to wonder why he'd been so keen to come on the school trip!

If this is all there is to it, I should have stayed at home, he thought.

The rushing, rumbling sound was louder now. Then Sam realised what the sound was and jerked with fear.

"Miss ... it's water!" Sam said as he turned to Mrs Tritton.

She frowned. "What?"

"It's …" Sam started to say, but he stopped as he heard something else.

"Help … Help me …"

The shout came from down below them. It sounded like Brandon's voice – gasping and frantic.

Mrs Tritton turned into the wind to slow herself down, and pushed further forward. Jack and Sam scrambled down after her. Sam was more on his bum than his feet as he slid down.

"Mrs Tritton, be careful," Sam shouted. "There's a river or something down there. That rumbling sound is water."

Sam's warning came just in time. Sam, Jack and Mrs Tritton slid to a stop just at the edge of a high bank, past the line of trees. If they'd gone half a metre more, they would have tumbled into the rushing water below them. That was what had happened to Brandon. Tayo was dangling from an over-hanging root at the edge of the bank. Tayo's feet were only centimetres above the water. Brandon was just below him, struggling to hold on to Tayo's leg with one hand. His other arm thrashed in the air. The raging river pulled at Brandon's legs and body, trying to pull him under.

"*Help* ..." Brandon yelled.

Brandon's head sank under the frothing, foaming water. When he surfaced again, coughing and spluttering, his eyes were huge with terror.

Above Brandon, Tayo kicked his legs around frantically as he tried to find a foothold. But, with each kick, Brandon's fingers slipped down Tayo's leg.

"Hold on, Tayo," Mrs Tritton said. "I'm coming, Brandon." She pulled off her anorak.

"Miss, you can't go down there," Jack said.

"Miss ... Miss, I'm falling," Tayo screamed. "Don't let me fall. *Don't let me fall!*"

The wind whipped around them, howling, roaring.

"Miss ..." Jack begged.

"I'll get Brandon, miss," Sam shouted. "You get Tayo."

"No, I should get Brandon," Mrs Tritton said.

"You can't," Sam told her. "Jack and I won't be able to pull Tayo up without going over ourselves. I'll help Brandon. I'll pull him out using my anorak."

"All right then," Mrs Tritton said. "Be careful, Sam. I'll be right here."

Sam nodded. "Hang on, Brandon. I'm coming," he shouted.

Sam stripped off his anorak fast, then his top jumper. He knotted one arm of the anorak to the left arm of the jumper. He pulled off his second jumper and knotted that to the right arm of the first jumper.

Mrs Tritton fell on to her front, so that her head and part of her upper body were over the edge of the bank.

"Jack, hold my ankles to stop me falling," Mrs Tritton ordered.

"Jack, give me your anorak first," Sam said.

Jack unzipped his anorak and pulled it off to give to Sam. Then Jack held on to Mrs Tritton's ankles as she reached over for Tayo.

Sam knotted Jack's anorak to his jumper. He was soaked and freezing. The rain kept running into his eyes, making him blink rapidly.

"Help me!" Brandon screamed, and his free arm thrashed faster.

Sam fell on to his front, next to Mrs Tritton.

"Brandon, grab hold of this," Sam shouted. He threw out his makeshift rope of anoraks and jumpers.

"Tayo, take my arm," Mrs Tritton called out.

The rope of clothes fell away from Brandon, and the rushing water tried to pull it from Sam's grip. It took every bit of Sam's strength to hang on to it.

"Sam ..." Brandon shouted.

Sam pulled the rope out of the river with a desperate jerk. He shuffled back slightly and threw the rope down again.

"Grab hold, Brandon," Sam pleaded.

He tried to swirl the rope of clothes closer to Brandon, but it was wet and heavy in his hands. It took all his strength to yank the rope over to Brandon.

Brandon swung his free hand out wildly and only just caught hold of it. Brandon let go of Tayo's leg and grasped the rope of anoraks and jumpers to him.

"That's it, Tayo," said Mrs Tritton. "Hold on, I'll pull you up. You're all right. You're safe. I won't let go of you."

Sam saw Mrs Tritton haul Tayo over the top of the bank and to safety.

"Can't ... can't hold it ..." Brandon said. His voice was getting weaker.

Brandon's fingers slipped down the rope. His head started going under the water. His face looked both desperate and resigned.

"Miss ... hold this," Sam said to Mrs Tritton, and he thrust the end of the makeshift rope into her hands. Sam stood up.

"*Sam, don't* ..." Mrs Tritton began to shout. But before she could say another word, Sam leaped into the water.

Chapter 10

What Are We Going to Do?

The moment Sam hit the freezing water, the whole world switched off. The howl of the wind and the rush of the river and the roar of the rain all vanished as Sam plunged downwards.

Sam could hear just one sound now. It took him a few moments to realise it was his heart hammering inside him. He puffed out his cheeks, pushed himself upwards with his hands and kicked with his legs. His lungs felt like they were bursting. Then he was gasping for air, with his head above the water. But now

Sam didn't have time to think about his lungs – or anything else. Brandon's head was almost all under the water. Sam reached out and shoved his hands under Brandon's armpits.

"I've ... I've g-got you, Brandon," Sam coughed and spluttered.

"Sam ... are you all right?" Mrs Tritton yelled out from above.

"Yeah ..." Sam called back. But he wasn't. He was having to kick like crazy to keep the river from washing him and Brandon away. He was exhausted. And so cold.

"Grab the anorak, Sam," Mrs Tritton shouted.

Sam had one hand holding Brandon's head above the water and snatched at his own anorak with the other. He reached it first time.

The water was less choppy now. The wind was dying down.

"Sam ..." Brandon whispered. His eyes were closed.

"Hang on, Brandon. I've got you," Sam said. But he knew that if he didn't get himself and Brandon out with his first try, then he wouldn't have the energy for a second attempt.

"Sam, tie the anorak around Brandon's waist," Mrs Tritton called.

Sam looked up. He could only see Mrs Tritton's head and one hand. The rest of her was hidden by the bank.

"Brandon, c-come on," Sam pleaded, his teeth chattering. "You've got to h-help me."

Slowly Brandon opened his eyes and said, "S-so cold ..."

Sam was too tired and too cold to reply. He had to conserve whatever energy he had left. He kicked hard to stay afloat as he passed the anorak around Brandon's back and tied it at the front. Sam raised his tired head and nodded at Mrs Tritton. Brandon's body began to move up out of the water as Mrs Tritton pulled on the rope. Sam waited until only Brandon's legs were still in the water and then let go of Brandon. Sam could hardly kick his legs at all now. He looked up. Brandon was being pulled over the bank. At least he was safe.

"Hold on, Sam," Tayo called out. "Just hold on."

But Sam wasn't sure he could hold on. He was so cold and oh, so tired. Every muscle in his body was screaming out for warmth and rest. Then a sharp stabbing pain shot into his stomach, making him gasp.

"Arrgh ..." Sam moaned. He wrapped his hands around his stomach as more pain arrowed into him. He sank under the water like a stone, with his hands clutched around his stomach. The water ran up his nose and down his throat and into his lungs, stinging and making him want to cough. Sam pushed out with his hands.

Right away, his head was above water again. He spluttered and retched, spitting out water. Sam scrambled to find some handhold in the steep bank. He was now about a metre further down. Sam saw Mrs Tritton pull the clothes rope out of the water and shuffle over on her front until her head was right above his.

"Grab the anorak, Sam," Mrs Tritton commanded.

The arm of the anorak hit the water just in front of Sam. He clutched the anorak to him.

"Hold on. We'll pull you up," Mrs Tritton shouted. "Don't let go, Sam."

The rain was now just a drizzle. The wind was more of a breeze. Sam clung to his anorak with both hands, his cheek pressed up to the cold, wet material. He kicked out with his legs to stop himself from swinging against the high bank.

Please don't hurt again. Please don't, Sam begged his stomach. He wouldn't be able to hold on if the pain in his stomach started up again.

Think of other things. Think of ...

There was no time to think of anything else. Sam felt many hands snatch at him and pull him over the bank. Sam lay on his stomach on the ground. He began coughing, and once he'd started he couldn't stop.

"Sam, don't you ever, *ever* do that again," Mrs Tritton said. "It was a very brave but stupid thing to do. You might have drowned." Mrs Tritton was so angry she was shaking.

Sam didn't answer. Mrs Tritton turned her head away.

"Are you OK?" Jack asked, worry in his voice.

Sam nodded. He had no energy to do anything else.

"Brandon … Brandon …" Sam whispered. He raised his head to look around for him.

"I'm f-fine," Brandon said. He was right next to Sam.

But Brandon didn't look fine. His face was pale and grey. His eyes were almost closed, and he was shivering violently.

"Let's cover Brandon and Sam with the anoraks and the jumpers," Mrs Tritton said. "Tayo, Jack, you wring out the jumpers first. They'll be damp, but they're better than nothing."

Mrs Tritton's face twisted as she tried to smile. But Sam could tell from the wild, haunted look in her eyes that Mrs Tritton was terrified. She'd been badly frightened and was frightened still. Drizzle ran slowly down her cheeks. Then Sam realised that it wasn't drizzle at all.

Brandon lay still while Tayo and Jack covered him from head to toe in the damp clothes.

"Miss ... I-I don't feel well," Brandon whispered.

"Don't worry, Brandon," Mrs Tritton said. "The other teachers must know that we're missing by now. They'll be out looking for us. So we'll soon be found, and then you'll be as right as rain in no time." But Mrs Tritton's voice was too jolly.

Sam looked at Tayo and Jack. They were thinking the same thing he was.

By now the teachers would know that the Green group were missing. But they hadn't followed Mrs Jenkins' route, so the teachers would be looking in the wrong place.

Mrs Tritton sat down with her back to the river. She wiped the water off her face. Tayo sat down next to her. Jack was the only one who stayed standing.

"I'm so glad everyone's safe," Mrs Tritton said. "I never want to go through that again. Never ever."

Sam sat up. His stomach was hurting … Not the sharp, stabbing pains of before, but a low constant ache which Sam knew all too well. He wasn't meant to get too hot or too cold or too dehydrated. If he did, he could have a sickle-cell crisis, and since they'd got off the coach he'd done all three. He knew what the stomach ache meant. And he knew from experience that it would get worse before it got better. A lot worse.

"Mrs Tritton, two of us should go for help," Sam forced himself to say.

"No way!" Mrs Tritton told him. "We all stay here together until we're found."

Sam looked at Brandon. His eyes were closed, and he didn't look good at all. Sam turned to Jack and Tayo.

I'm going to tell her, Sam thought. *If one of you doesn't, then I will.*

"Mrs Tritton ... we have to go for help," Tayo said. He lowered his head as he spoke. "We ... well, we wanted to get to the meeting place first, so we changed our route on the map to cut through the woods."

"But I saw the map ..." Mrs Tritton began.

"We got our map with the real route on it last week," Jack said. "We bought another one from the hotel this morning and drew in our new route. We wanted to be first."

Mrs Tritton stared at Jack. She turned her head to stare at all of them.

"Is this true?" she asked.

Jack nodded. Sam looked right at her.

"Yes, miss," Tayo mumbled.

Mrs Tritton took a deep breath and said, "I see."

"We didn't mean for all this to happen, Mrs Tritton," Tayo said. "Honest, we didn't."

"Of course you didn't," Mrs Tritton replied. "But that's not the most important thing at the moment." She looked up at the steep hill in front of her. "What's important is, what are we going to do now?"

Chapter 11

Trouble

"Mrs Tritton, I don't ... I don't ..." Brandon whispered. Then his eyes closed and his head rolled to one side.

Mrs Tritton was beside him in a flash.

"Brandon!" Tayo said, and ran over to him.

Mrs Tritton took Brandon's pulse, then checked his breathing.

"Brandon! *Brandon, wake up!*" Mrs Tritton shouted. She shook Brandon, and his eyelids fluttered open. "Brandon, stay awake. Don't go to sleep."

"I can't help it. I'm so tired," Brandon whispered.

"Brandon, stay awake," Mrs Tritton said, and she shook him again.

Brandon nodded, but his eyelids kept drooping.

"We're way off the route, Mrs Tritton," Sam said. "If we'd followed the path, we would have been south-west of the meeting place most of the time – but we're south-east. So if anyone is looking for us, they'll start in the wrong place. Two of us have to go and get help."

"But which two? We're all exhausted," Mrs Tritton said.

"I'll go," Sam said. He pushed the damp jumper and anorak off his body and wrung them out.

"I'll go with you," said Jack.

"Will you be able to find your way?" Mrs Tritton asked. "Will you be able to make it up the hill alone? I don't want to leave Brandon."

"I don't want to go up that hill again," Jack said.

Sam dug a hand into his soaked trouser pockets. He took out his compass. The needle was swimming in a pool of water.

"My compass is no good any more," Sam said. "We'll need the other one."

Tayo dug into his anorak pocket and pulled out the compass. He handed it over. Mrs Tritton stood up.

"Tayo, keep an eye on Brandon," Mrs Tritton said. "Don't let him fall asleep. I want a word with Jack and Sam."

She walked over to them with her back towards Tayo and Brandon and her expression set.

"I hate the idea of sending you off to get help, but I can't leave Brandon," Mrs Tritton said. "He's going into shock, and if we're not careful ..." She swallowed hard. "So I want the two of you to take this map and the compass. You have to go up the hill and then head west." Mrs Tritton moved to stand between Sam and Jack. She pointed down at the map in her hand and brushed water droplets off the clear plastic bag around it. "If you steer west, you should come across this path."

"But how will we know if we're north or south of the meeting point?" Jack asked.

"By the contour lines," Sam said, and he pointed. "Look! They're closer together north of the meeting place, which means that area is hilly – it must be the bit we're on now. If we use the map and the compass to make sure we travel south-west, we should get to the meeting place."

"That's right," Mrs Tritton said. "Now are you both sure you know how to read the compass?"

Sam nodded first. Jack's nod took longer.

"Mrs Tritton," Tayo called. "Brandon's drifted off again." Tayo's voice was full of panic.

Mrs Tritton turned and ran back to Brandon.

"Come on, Jack," Sam said. "Let's get going." Sam started back up the hill.

"Sam and Jack," Mrs Tritton called out to them.

The two boys turned.

"Good luck," Mrs Tritton told them. She looked down at Brandon before raising her head to them again. "Bring help back – soon ..."

Sam didn't say another word and started to climb the hill. Jack joined him. Now that the wind had died down, it was easier to get up it. The rain was just a drizzle. Not that it made much difference. Sam couldn't have been much wetter. Or colder. Every time the wind blew against Sam's wet jumper, it felt like he had an ice-pack on his chest.

"Hang on, you two," Tayo shouted as he ran up to them and pulled off his anorak. "Here you are, Sam. Let's swap coats. Mine's dry."

"But what about you?" Sam asked.

"You need it more than I do," Tayo replied.

"Meaning what?" Sam frowned.

"Meaning you're the one who went in the river, not me," said Tayo.

For a second, Sam thought about arguing, but Tayo thrust the coat into his hands and pulled off Sam's damp one. Tayo ran back to Brandon and Mrs Tritton before Sam could say another word. Sam looked at Tayo's coat, then put it on. He and Jack kept on walking.

"I'm tired already," Jack said.

Sam nodded to agree. He was too tired even to talk. His stomach was beginning to hurt again. Not so bad as to double him over, but he was very aware that a sickle-cell crisis was starting. He could take only shallow breaths now. If he tried to take a deep breath, his stomach stabbed like the jab of a red-hot knife. It was like having a really bad stitch that wouldn't ease. Sam stopped for a moment, took a slow, deep breath and let it out just as slowly. He had to do this. Brandon was depending on him. They all were. Today, Sam wasn't going to be ruled by his body.

"What's the matter?" Jack asked.

Sam shook his head and kept on walking. For every two steps they took up the hill, they slid back down one step. But at long last they reached the top.

"Which way now?" Jack asked.

Sam dug out the compass and the map just to make sure. "I think we're here now," Sam said, and pointed. "So if we head along the top of this hill, then down, we should reach a clearing with a path."

"What about this way?" Jack said, and drew his finger across the map. "Can't we take a shortcut through the trees?"

Sam looked right at him and said, "I don't know about you, but I've had enough of shortcuts to last me a lifetime."

Jack paused and then said, "Along the hill it is."

Sam gave a small smile, which Jack returned.

They set off along the ridge of the hill in silence. Fifteen minutes later, they had reached the bottom of the hill and were standing in a clearing. The hill was behind them, and there were trees everywhere else. By this time even the drizzle had died away, but the ground was still slippery and difficult to walk on.

"Are we lost again?" Jack whispered.

Sam shook his head hard. "No, we can't be. We followed the compass and the map. And this *is* the clearing."

"Then where's the path?" Jack asked.

Sam looked around, feeling desperate. Jack was right. There was no path in sight. But there had to be. There just *had* to be. Because Sam wasn't sure how much longer he could last. The ache in his stomach was a lot worse and now, on top of everything, he was getting a pain in his hip as well.

"So where's the path?" Jack said. "Where's the path?"

"Jack, calm down," Sam said. He held his breath, trying to control the pain that seemed to be creeping all over his body. There was no doubt about it – he was having a sickle-cell crisis. He had to keep going. He couldn't give in. Sam let out a breath and spoke at the same time. "The path must be around here somewhere."

"I can't see it," Jack said. His voice was getting higher.

Jack started to run to the closest clump of trees. Sam tried to run after him, but after five steps he knew he couldn't take another. If Sam didn't stop Jack from panicking – and fast – Jack would run off and leave him.

Chapter 12

Angry Monster

"*Jack. No. Stop!*" Sam called out. "Look! The path is that way." He pointed wildly another way. Sam couldn't see a path, but he was desperate to stop Jack from running off.

It worked. Jack stopped and asked, "The path? You can see it?"

Sam nodded. "Yes, it's just past those trees."

Jack walked slowly back to Sam.

Sam didn't speak. What was there to say?

"You really saw it?" Jack asked as he looked the way Sam had pointed.

Sam nodded. Jack strode off and Sam followed, all the while trying to come up with a plan to keep Jack from running off again. Because Sam was hurting – really hurting – now. His stomach was on fire, like white-hot needles were being jabbed into him. And his hip was aching so much he could hardly walk.

They were at the edge of the trees.

Jack looked around, frowning as he searched for the path. Sam tried to think of something to say. He couldn't be on his own. And he didn't want to tell Jack just how close he was to collapsing. Sam couldn't show Tayo and Brandon and all the others in his class that they had been right. They all thought he was the world's biggest wimp. If he quit now, if he keeled over, they would never let him forget it. But he couldn't last much longer.

"I see it! I see it!" Jack yelled, and darted deeper into the trees. Sam followed him as best he could, but he was unable to run.

"Sam, you were right," Jack said. "There is a path. Look! *Look!*"

And there it was – a path leading away from them. Sam had never seen anything that made him so happy.

"How on earth did you see this from the clearing back there?" Jack asked, impressed.

Sam shrugged and said, "I ... I just have great eyes, that's all."

He was going to tell Jack the truth but decided not to. They weren't out of the woods yet! Maybe Sam would tell him when they were all safe and sound.

"Let's go," Jack said. He started running along the path.

Sam tried his best to keep up but couldn't. It took all of his strength just to put one foot in front of the other.

"Come on, Sam," Jack called back after him. "What are you waiting for? Let's go!"

"I'm going as fast as I can," Sam hissed.

Jack stopped and turned around to frown at Sam. "You're not feeling too well, are you?"

Sam shook his head.

"Why didn't you say so before?" Jack asked. He walked back to Sam and said, "Do you want to lean on me?"

"No, thanks," Sam gasped out.

"Don't be stupid," Jack said. He put Sam's arm around his back. "You're not a wimp just because you need some help."

"That's not what you and your friends have been saying all term," Sam said. He couldn't stop his voice sounding bitter.

Jack turned his head away, looking embarrassed. "We didn't mean it," he said. "It didn't mean anything."

"It did to me," Sam replied.

Jack looked at him. "I'm sorry."

Sam was silent, then said, "We'd better get going."

And they followed the path deeper into the woods.

As Sam couldn't walk very fast, their progress was slow. And Sam found himself having to lean more and more on Jack. Soon Jack was breathing hard, with sweat dripping off his forehead like heavy rain off an umbrella.

Sam steered them towards a tree. He leaned against it and closed his eyes until he had his breath back.

"I think you'd better go on without me," Sam said. "I'm just slowing you down."

"No way," Jack replied at once. "We both go on or we both stop here."

"Don't be stupid," said Sam. "I've had it. I can't take another step."

"Then I won't," Jack insisted.

Sam scowled at him. "Don't you understand? My hip hurts and my stomach hurts and my head hurts. I can't walk any more."

"Your stomach and your hip have been hurting for ages," Jack said. "But you didn't let it stop you from going for help, did you?"

Sam stared at Jack and asked, "How did you know I was hurting?"

Jack looked even more embarrassed than earlier. "Mariella has the same thing as you – sickle-cell," Jack said.

"Mariella?" Sam asked.

"My sister-in-law," said Jack. "She's from Italy."

A thought came into Sam's head before he could stop it: *All that time, all that time you knew what I've been going through and you still made my life a misery.* Sam wasn't just thinking about today in the forest but about the weeks and months that Jack had stood by and let his friends tease Sam. Sam could see from the look on Jack's face that he had guessed what he was thinking.

"I'm really sorry," Jack said again.

"Yeah, right," Sam replied.

"Yes, I am," Jack insisted. "I should have said something. I could have said something, only ..."

"Only what?" Sam demanded.

"Only I—"

Jack was cut off by the sound of a distant whistle. Sam and Jack turned their heads.

"Did you hear that?" Sam whispered.

Jack nodded and said, "It came from over there somewhere."

BRREEEPPP! There it was again. Jack took out his whistle and blew it so hard that the sound shot through Sam's head and made his ears ring. Jack blew it again. And again.

"Stop. Stop!" Sam yelled.

Sam put out his hand to stop Jack from blowing the whistle any more.

"But—" Jack started to say.

"Let's see if they've heard us before you blow it any more," Sam said.

The two boys listened. Silence at first. Then a much louder whistle. Followed by another one and another one. And the sound was getting closer and closer.

"They found us," Jack said. "They found us!" He jumped up and down.

Sam tried to push himself away from the tree trunk, but pain sliced into him and he doubled over.

"Hang on, Sam," Jack told him. "They've found us."

Jack took Sam's arm and tried to help him stand up.

But Sam couldn't. The pain now was worse than it'd ever been. So bad that he couldn't breathe. So bad that he couldn't even think. His whole body was in pain.

"Sam, please," Jack said. "Sam ..."

Jack's voice was being drowned out by the blood roaring in Sam's ears.

There was no sound now but his blood roaring like some angry monster. Sam fell to his knees, still clutching his stomach. Everything around him was spinning fast. Then he fell forward, feeling thankful that the world was fading into dark nothingness.

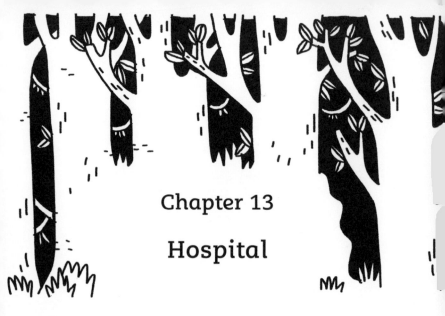

Chapter 13

Hospital

Sam knew that smell. He knew the sounds too.
But still he crossed his fingers and kept his
eyes shut.

Please let me be wrong, he thought. *Please
don't let me be in hospital.*

Slowly, Sam opened his eyes. He wasn't
wrong. He lay in a hospital bed, and beside him
were his mum and dad.

Sam closed his eyes again. That was that,
then. So much for his first – and his last –

school trip. He pulled the oxygen mask off his face.

"I suppose you'll never let me out of your sight again," he said.

"Hello to you too!" Mum said, and raised her eyebrows.

"For now, we just want you to focus on getting well," Dad chipped in. "So put your mask back on."

"There'll be plenty of time to discuss all this when we get home," said Mum.

Sam looked from his mum to his dad and back again. "No. I want to discuss it now."

"Sam ..." Dad said.

"It wasn't my fault," Sam said as he struggled to sit up. The drip running into his right arm and the pump and tube attached to his left arm made it difficult for him to move.

"Sam, I really think ..." Mum began.

"Mum, it wasn't my fault," Sam said. "We got lost and Brandon fell in the river and I had to help him. That's why I got ill. It wasn't the rain or the wind or anything. It's because I got cold in the river."

"Yes, I know, dear," Mum said. "Now just lie back." Mum was gentle but insistent as she made Sam lie back on his pillows.

"You're not listening to me," Sam realised as his hopes of explaining faded.

"We heard every word," Mum said with a smile. "You're the one not listening to us. I just told you that we know all about it. Jack, Mrs Tritton and your friend Brandon have told us all about how you saved them. We've even had the local newspapers asking us if they can interview you."

Sam stared at his mum. He was stunned. He didn't understand a lot of what she'd just said. "I didn't save anyone," Sam told her.

Dad smiled and said, "That's not what your friend here said."

"Pardon?" Sam replied.

Dad stepped to one side so that Sam could see who was in the next bed. It was Brandon, grinning at him.

"Hi, Sam," Brandon said. "How're you feeling now?"

"What ... what're you doing here?" Sam asked.

"I've got exposure and mild hypothermia," Brandon told Sam. "I should be able to leave the day after tomorrow." Brandon shrugged. "Do you know how long you'll be stuck in here for?"

"No idea," Sam said, and shook his head. "But I feel fine now."

Sam couldn't take it in. Mum and Dad kept calling Brandon his friend, and Brandon wasn't arguing. Maybe Sam should correct them, but he was reluctant to do so.

"What about Tayo and Jack and Mrs Tritton?" Sam asked. "Are they all OK?"

"They're fine," Brandon assured him. "But we're all in big trouble. Mrs Jenkins has said that as soon as we're all back at school she wants to talk to us – and you know what that means. Mrs Jenkins' talks can last for days."

Sam wondered if Mrs Jenkins' "us" meant Sam as well. He hoped so. He really hoped so.

"I think you're going to be in trouble for not telling Mrs Jenkins what the rest of us were up to," Brandon said.

Sam smiled to show his relief. Brandon smiled back.

"You OK?" Sam asked.

"I'm fine," Brandon said. He lay back in the bed, his face looking tired in spite of his words. "Oh, and Sam?"

"Yes?" Sam said.

"Thanks for saving my life."

"You're welcome."

"Well done, Sam," said Dad. "You were very brave."

"I collapsed before help arrived," Sam sighed.

"But you were fantastic," Mum said. "Everyone's told us so. You did great."

"Yes, I did, didn't I?" Sam agreed.

His mum and dad started laughing at that.

Sam smiled and added, "If the next school trip is as action-packed as this one, I'm going to have a great time."

"Er, Sam," Mum said. "If the next school trip looks like being as … *busy* as this one, promise me something."

"What?" Sam asked.

"That you'll write us a postcard warning your dad and me first!" Mum said.

Sam decided to take the chance to tell his parents something else. "When I get back to school, I think I'll try out for the football team," Sam said. "I'm a pretty good goalie."

"You'll get selected – no trouble," Dad said.

Sam held his breath as he looked at his mum, waiting for her answer.

"Go get 'em!" Mum said.

"I will," Sam laughed. "You just watch me!"

And in that moment Sam knew that everything was going to be OK. He still had sickle-cell anaemia, and it wasn't going to go away. But it wasn't going to stop him from doing the things he wanted to do any longer.

"This has been the best school trip ever," Sam sighed as he settled back down on his pillows. "Because now I know for sure there isn't a thing in this world I can't do if I try."

"What's he talking about?" Brandon asked.

"He's just wittering," Mum said, and shook her head. "He's had too much river water, I think."

And that was the last thing Sam heard before he fell asleep.

Author's Note

Sickle-Cell Disease

Sickle-Cell Disease (SCD) is an inherited disorder that people have from birth – it is passed to a child by both parents. It is not contagious – you can't catch it from someone else like a cold or the flu. Both parents must have the sickle-cell gene for there to be a chance that their child will have SCD.

Red blood cells carry oxygen around the body to all the organs and tissues that need it. These cells are soft and shaped like doughnuts – discs with the middle partly scooped out – and move easily in our small blood vessels.

SCD causes red blood cells to be different. They are shaped like crescent moons or sickles (hence the name) and tend to clump together. This makes these cells stiff and more fragile. These sickle cells don't move around the bloodstream easily and can block blood vessels. When this happens, the body's organs and tissues don't get the oxygen they need to stay healthy. This leads to terrible pain, which is known as a sickle-cell crisis. Sometimes this means the person has to go into hospital to receive strong pain relief, oxygen and perhaps even a blood transfusion.

It's also common for people with SCD to have trouble fighting infections and to become very tired, because their body isn't getting the oxygen it needs. They must be careful not to get too hot, too cold, too dehydrated or too stressed, as any of these things can lead to a sickle-cell crisis.

You can find out more about SCD on the Sickle Cell Society website: **www.sicklecellsociety.org**

Our books are tested
for children and young people by
children and young people.

Thanks to everyone who consulted on
a manuscript for their time and effort in
helping us to make our books better
for our readers.